SURREALISM

★ IN MY GALLERY ★

WRITTEN BY

DESIGNED BY

Published in 2022 by Enslow Publishing, LLC
101 W. 23rd Street, Suite 240,
New York, NY 10011

Copyright © 2020 Booklife Publishing
This edition published by arrangement with Booklife Publishing

All rights reserved.

No part of this book may be reproduced by any means without the written permission of the publisher.

Cataloging-in-Publication Data

Names: Dufresne, Emilie.
Title: Surrealism / Emilie Dufresne.
Description: New York : Enslow Publishing, 2022. | Series: In my gallery | Includes glossary and index.
Identifiers: ISBN 9781978524231 (pbk.) | ISBN 9781978524255 (library bound) | ISBN 9781978524248 (6 pack) | ISBN 9781978524262 (ebook)
Subjects: LCSH: Surrealism--Juvenile literature. | Arts, Modern--20th century--Juvenile literature.
Classification: LCC NX456.5.S8 D843 2022 | DDC 709.04'063--dc23

Designer: Danielle Rippengill
Editor: Madeline Tyler

Printed in the United States of America

CPSIA compliance information: Batch #CS22ENS: For further information contact Enslow Publishing, New York, New York at 1-800-398-2504

IMAGE CREDITS

Cover and throughout - Artbesouro, April_pie, Shtonado, Tashanatasha, Quarta, Aratehortua, Lukpedclub, Delcarmat, IhorZIGOR, Display Intermaya, Vectorok. Backgrounds - ExpressVectors. Hema & Artists - Grinbox. Gallery - GoodStudio, Siberian Art. 2 - Focus_Bell, GST. 5 - Glinskaja Olga, Stockvector. 8 - Mastak A. 9 - Graphic Design, Mei Yanotai, Jason Winter, Lera Efremova. 10 - Lucky Team Studio, Cepera. 11 - Delcarmat. 14&15 - Delcarmat, Thebirdss. 18&19 - Doloves, Aratehortua, Mr. Luck. 22&23 - Dharmast, Kateryna Artemieva. 26&27 - Focus_Bell, GST. 28 - Doloves, Aratehortua, Mr. Luck, Delcarmat, Thebirdss. 29 - Focus_Bell, GST, Dharmast, Kateryna Artemieva. Images are courtesy of shutterstock.com. With thanks to Getty Images, Thinkstock Photo, and iStockphoto.

CONTENTS

Page 4	Welcome to the Gallery
Page 5	Types of Art
Page 6	Surrealism Wing
Page 8	What Is Surrealism?
Page 12	René Magritte
Page 14	Activity: Fruit Face
Page 16	Salvador Dalí
Page 18	Activity: Weird Objects
Page 20	Frida Kahlo
Page 22	Activity: Animal Self-Portrait
Page 24	Li Wei
Page 26	Activity: Trick Photography
Page 28	Opening Night
Page 30	Quiz
Page 31	Glossary
Page 32	Index

Words that look like **this** are explained in the glossary on page 31.

WELCOME TO THE GALLERY

Hi, I'm Hema! I work in this gallery and I am putting together an exhibition all about Surrealism. Do you want to learn all about galleries and art? I will need your help to get all these artworks finished in time for opening night.

Museums and Galleries

Museums and galleries buy, or are given, artworks or **artifacts** that they take care of, repair, and show to the public. Museums and galleries allow us to go to see art, whether it was created hundreds of years ago or just yesterday. Have you ever been to a museum or gallery?

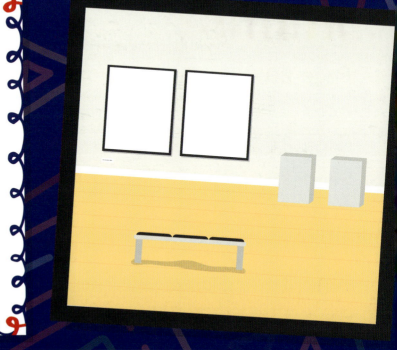

TYPES OF ART

Art can be made in lots of different ways. Let's learn some more about the types of art we will see in this book.

Painting is when paint is put onto a surface. There are many different types of paint, including **acrylic** and **watercolor**. Paint can be put onto a surface using tools such as brushes, sponges, or trowels.

Assemblage is when different objects are put together to create a piece of art that might look like an **installation** or **sculpture**. Salvador Dalí was known for putting objects together to create assemblage art.

Photography is a type of art where a camera is used to take photos. These photos can be of anything, including people and **landscapes**. Li Wei uses cameras to create his art.

5

SURREALISM WING

Here it is – the Surrealism Wing! Soon, all these empty spaces will be filled with art created in the style of Surrealism.

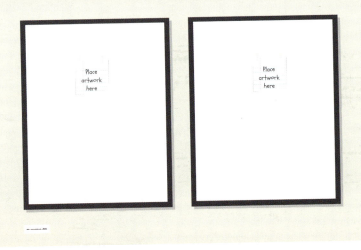

Often, there are lots of different areas in a museum or gallery. Each area might show art from a specific artist, time period, or **movement**. This gallery has different wings for different movements.

This wing is going to be one of the strangest and most dreamlike wings in the gallery. We could have some extraordinary assemblages on those stands, and some preposterous paintings and mind-boggling photographs on this wall here.

Let's find out more about the Surrealism movement.

SURREALISM CAN MEAN "BEYOND WHAT IS REAL." FOR EXAMPLE, IN SURREALISM, THINGS MIGHT BE SHOWN TOGETHER THAT WOULDN'T NORMALLY BE SHOWN TOGETHER. THIS MAKES THE ART SEEM AS THOUGH IT COULD BE STRAIGHT OUT OF THE WILDEST OF DREAMS.

WHAT IS SURREALISM?

Before Surrealism

Surrealism started in the 1920s, but this wasn't when art started getting strange. Before Surrealism, there was Dada. Dada artists wanted to break away from traditional ways of making art. They didn't believe that art had to make sense and often made fun of earlier ways of making art.

DADA ART WAS VERY CONTROVERSIAL, BUT SURREALISM WAS ABOUT TO TAKE ART TO A WHOLE NEW LEVEL OF WEIRD AND WONDERFUL...

Dada artists created art in strange ways. Marcel Duchamp was a Dada artist. He took a urinal and turned it on its side. He signed it and said it was now a sculpture with the name *Fountain*. Duchamp also made a piece of art in which he gave the *Mona Lisa* a mustache.

After the War

Dada and Surrealism came after **World War I**, which ended in 1918. It is thought that Dada was a **reaction** to the war. Artists found it hard to show what was happening in the world because of the damage and pain the war had caused.

DADA ARTWORK

A Nonsense World

Dada artists also felt that the world before and during the war did not make sense anymore. They wanted to **protest** against that world because it led them into a terrible war. This is why Dada art didn't seem to make sense and didn't look like any type of art that had been made before.

Curiouser and Curiouser

Surrealism began in the mid-1920s and was **influenced** by Dada. Surrealist artists wanted to question the way many people thought about the world and make imagination more important than what was real. If your mind could think it, it could become Surrealist art, even if it didn't make sense or exist in real life.

SURREALIST ARTWORK

Lose Yourself

Some Surrealist artists tried to lose themselves in thought. They didn't want to control what their minds were thinking of and instead tried to get lost in them. This helped them to create weird and wonderful art. For example, André Masson was a Surrealist artist who created drawings by moving his pen around the page quickly, not taking it off the paper until a picture formed.

HAVE YOU EVER HAD A DREAM WHERE SOMETHING SEEMED A LITTLE STRANGE?

Dreams and Nightmares

Surrealist artists often created artworks that might make you feel as though you were in a dream or nightmare. When looking at Surrealist art, you might recognize certain objects, but they might be the wrong size, a different **texture**, or even in completely the wrong place.

Mix and Match

When two things don't look like they should be put together, it is called juxtaposition. Surrealist artists often made juxtapositions to make people think about why those things were shown that way. It could also make people feel uneasy, or as though something wasn't quite right.

RENÉ MAGRITTE

Country of Birth: Belgium
Born: 1898
Died: 1967 (aged 68)

René Magritte was born in Belgium. He moved to Paris in the 1920s, and this is where his **career** as an artist really took off. Magritte's artistic style was slightly different than the other Surrealist artists of the time. Instead of making confusing and dreamlike paintings, Magritte took everyday objects and put them in situations you wouldn't normally expect. His paintings would often show things such as people, clouds, and cities, but these would often be shown in strange ways.

For example, Magritte painted pictures of men with their faces missing, with fruit in front of their faces, or wearing floating hats on their heads. One of his most famous paintings was of a pipe. Under the pipe Magritte wrote: "This is not a pipe." Many people still talk about what Magritte meant by this.

Activity:
FRUIT FACE

You will need:

Paintbrushes ☑

Pencils ☑

Paint in different colors ☑

Thick paper or cardboard ☑

Let's make a painting in the style of Magritte. I really like the paintings where he paints people as having fruit for a face. Let's try that!

Take your paper or cardboard and **sketch** a drawing of how you want your picture to look.

I have chosen a watermelon, but you could use an orange, kiwifruit, or any other fruit.

Magritte painted a lot of people wearing hats, so I am going to draw my person wearing a hat.

It's time to paint on top of your sketch. Think about what colors you want the person's clothes to be and what could be in the background of your picture.

I have chosen to put a blue sky and clouds in the background of mine. But your background can be of anything. You could even paint your fruit an unusual color. Your picture can be as weird and as wonderful as you want it to be!

15

SALVADOR DALÍ

Country of Birth: Spain
Born: 1904
Died: 1989 (aged 84)

Salvador Dalí is one of the most famous artists from the Surrealist movement. He worked in many different types of art, including painting and assemblage. Before he began creating Surrealist work, he had experimented with **Impressionism**, **Cubism**, and other types of art.

On a trip to Paris, he made friends with other artists who were creating Surrealist work. Soon, he too began creating Surrealist art. His paintings often showed dreamlike scenes which looked like real life. This made it easy for people to step into the weird and wonderful world of Dalí's imagination. One of his most famous paintings, *The Persistence of Memory,* shows large melting clocks in a **barren** landscape. Dalí also created assemblages of weird objects such as lobsters on telephones.

Dalí was even surreal in how he lived his life. He once went to an exhibition dressed in a full diving suit to show how his art wanted to dive into the human mind.

17

Activity:
WEIRD OBJECTS

You will need:

A selection of toys ☑

Five random objects ☑

A cardboard box ☑

White paint ☑

A paintbrush ☑

It is time to make an assemblage like Dalí.

Remember to ask permission before taking objects to use in your artwork.

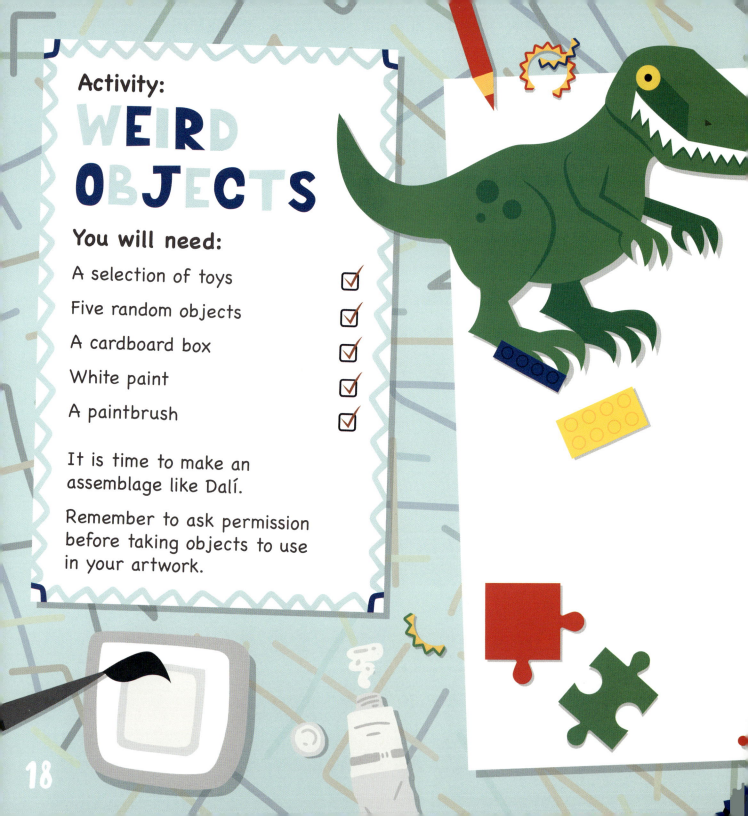

Paint your cardboard box white and leave it to dry. This will give you somewhere to display your assemblage.

Try putting some of your objects together. They don't have to look as though they match.

Maybe you could put a watch over an apple, or fill a pair of shoes with a building block tower.

Keep playing around with your objects until you have a weird and wonderful assemblage.

I think I am nearly done. I want to use this old phone and this toy dinosaur.

Once your assemblage is done, put it on the box and there you have it – your very own work in the style of Dalí!

FRIDA KAHLO

Country of Birth: Mexico
Born: 1907
Died: 1954 (aged 47)

Frida Kahlo was badly injured in a bus accident as a child, so she spent a lot of her time in the hospital having operations. In her paintings, she tried to show how her body felt and how she saw herself. Kahlo painted many portraits of herself in different situations.

Kahlo would often paint herself wearing ribbons as well as having facial hair on her upper lip and eyebrows. Through these portraits, she explored what it meant to be a woman. Kahlo did not see herself as a Surrealist artist. To Kahlo, her paintings showed how she experienced real life. Many people see her paintings as Surrealist because they often showed unusual images in strange situations.

Kahlo was known for her portraits in which she showed herself with animals and plants. In one painting, *The Wounded Deer*, Kahlo painted a deer with her face on it.

Activity:
ANIMAL SELF-PORTRAIT

You will need:

- Drawing pencils ☑
- Colored pencils ☑
- Thick paper or cardboard ☑
- An eraser ☑

Kahlo often painted herself with animals and plants that she felt **represented** her **heritage** or **culture**.

Let's try to paint a self-portrait that represents ourselves.

22

Think about what animals and plants you feel represent you.

I have chosen my favorite plant, the passionflower, and my favorite animal, a cat.

Using a pencil, sketch yourself and include the items you want around you. At the front of the picture I sketched myself with a cat around my shoulders and I added passionflowers into the background.

Now, use the colored pencils to bring your sketch to life.

I used bright colors for my flowers, and I used my favorite color, orange, for the cat – just like my cat at home!

What colors will you use?

23

LI WEI

Country of Birth: China
Born: 1970

Li Wei is a <u>contemporary</u> artist. He has created many different types of art, including <u>performance art</u> and photography. His photography often includes Wei himself in amazing situations that look too dangerous to be real, such as hanging off the edges of buildings, floating in midair, or sticking headfirst out of a building. Wei creates these strange photographs using just his body and a few other objects.

Wei is seen as a Contemporary Surrealist artist because his work creates dreamlike situations, much like the Surrealists in the 1900s. However, he does this in a contemporary way by using photography and modern places and objects.

Wei creates his photographs using very clever tricks to make the situations look impossible or dangerous, even though they really aren't. He doesn't edit the photos using computers, but he does use hidden wires and his own body to create his mind-boggling photographs.

Activity:
TRICK PHOTOGRAPHY

You will need:

- A camera ☑
- Paper ☑
- A printer ☑
- Scissors ☑
- Glue ☑
- Thick paper or cardboard ☑

We don't have any cranes or wires to help us create Surrealist photography, so we will just have to get creative. Let's get snapping!

26

I think I'm going to try to create a Surrealist photograph of a giant version of me climbing really high up in a tree. I will need to get some photos of trees and of me looking as though I'm climbing.

Think about what mind-boggling photo you want to create and then take photos of the things you need for it. You could do this at your local park or at home.

Print your photos and cut out the parts you need. I have cut out a picture of me and some pictures of trees. Arrange your photographs onto the thick paper or cardboard until you are happy with how your trick photo looks. Then glue the photos down. There you go – your very own Surrealist photograph!

OPENING NIGHT

All the Surrealist artworks are finished and in the gallery. Everything looks great! I wonder what everyone thinks of our artworks. Let's see...

It is fun to talk about art because everyone has different opinions. Look at the art you have created and try to answer these questions. Which is your favorite piece? Why is it your favorite? What do you like most about it?

QUIZ

1. Name a type of art that came before Surrealism.
2. Which artist created a piece called *Fountain*?
3. What technique did Dalí use to make his Surrealist sculptures?
4. Which artist often painted themselves with animals, ribbons, and facial hair?
5. What country was Li Wei born in?

Answers: 1. Dada, 2. Marcel Duchamp, 3. Assemblage, 4. Frida Kahlo, 5. China

Are there any museums or galleries near you that you could visit?

They will have lots of artworks and artifacts for you to look at. You could try to discuss how the art makes you feel and whether you like it or not. Ask the people you are with what they think. It is interesting to see how differently people can see one piece of art.

GLOSSARY

acrylic	a type of fast-drying paint
artifacts	objects made by humans in history
barren	not able to produce or support the growth of crops
career	a job, or set of jobs, that a person has for a long time
contemporary	belonging to the current time period
controversial	something that causes public disagreement
Cubism	an art movement in which people and objects were represented through geometric shapes such as cubes
culture	the traditions, ideas, and ways of life of a particular group of people
heritage	the culture, traditions, and ideas that might come from a person's background, which can include their family or the place they live
Impressionism	an art movement that aimed to give the impression of movement through light and color
influenced	to have had an effect on the behavior of someone or something
installation	a piece of art that people have to interact with by walking around, touching, or listening to
landscapes	scenes that include nature such as fields, mountains, or oceans
movement	a category or type of art that an artwork or artist might belong to, which can sometimes be related to a certain time or place
performance art	a type of art that is often performed live to viewers or spectators
protest	an action that shows disagreement toward something
reaction	something done in response to something else
represented	acted as a symbol for something else
sculpture	a decorative object made by carving, chiseling, or molding
sketch	to do a quick drawing, often in pencil
texture	the feel or look of something
traditional	related to very old behaviors or beliefs
urinal	a bowl or a toilet that is used for collecting and taking away urine
watercolor	a type of paint that can be mixed with water
World War I	a war fought between 1914 and 1918

INDEX

A
animals 16, 20, 22–23
artifacts 4, 30
assemblage 5, 7, 16, 18–19

C
Cubism 16

D
Dada 8–10
dreams 7, 11–12, 16, 24
Duchamp, Marcel 8

G
galleries 4, 6–7, 28, 30

I
Impressionism 16
installations 5

J
juxtapositions 11

M
Masson, André 10
museums 4, 6, 30

P
painting 5, 7, 12, 14–16, 20, 22
performance art 24
photography 5, 7, 24, 26–27, 29
portraits 20, 22–23

S
sculpture 5, 8
sketching 15, 23

W
World War I 9

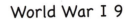

32